Lands of The Silk Road
Ninth Century

UIGHURS

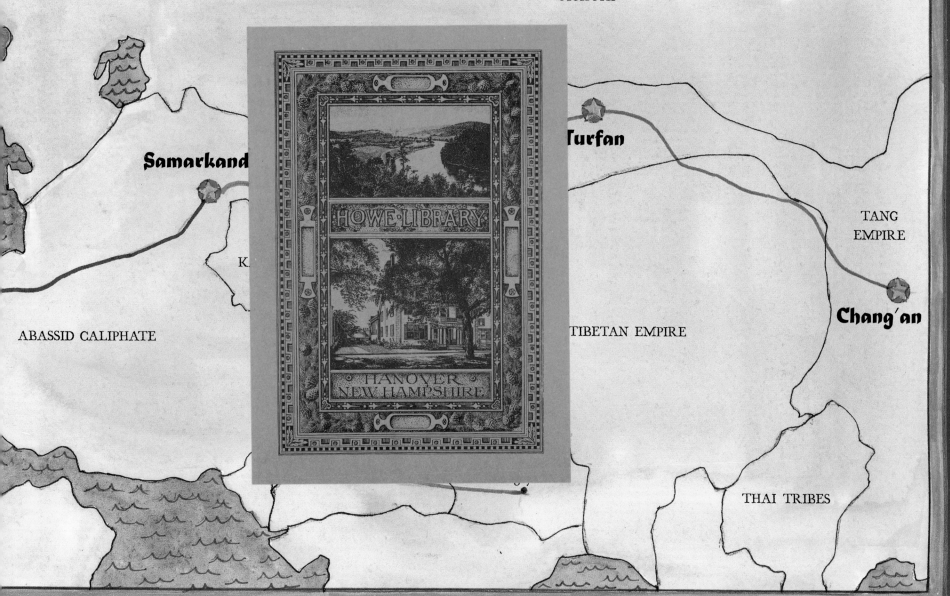

HOWE·LIBRARY

HANOVER
NEW HAMPSHIRE

Samarkand

Turfan

TANG
EMPIRE

K.

ABASSID CALIPHATE

TIBETAN EMPIRE

Chang'an

THAI TRIBES

A Single Pebble

A STORY OF THE SILK ROAD

BONNIE CHRISTENSEN

A NEAL PORTER BOOK
ROARING BROOK PRESS
NEW YORK

For Emily

And for travellers everywhere, for those who dream of travelling, and for collectors of pebbles.

Many thanks to Neal, Jennifer, and Marcia for putting this story on the road,
to Andrea for historical guidance, to Leda for reading many versions, to Lily,
and to Ponnie Wessel's class at Sallie B. Howard School for listening with enthusiasm.

Copyright © 2013 by Bonnie Christensen

A Neal Porter Book

Published by Roaring Brook Press

Roaring Brook Press is a division of Holtzbrinck Publishing Holdings Limited Partnership

175 Fifth Avenue, New York, New York 10010

mackids.com

Library of Congress Cataloging-in-Publication Data

Christensen, Bonnie, author, illustrator.

A single pebble : a story of the Silk Road / Bonnie Christensen. —
First edition.

pages cm

"A Neal Porter Book."

Summary: "In 9th century China, a little girl sends a small jade pebble
to travel with her father along the Silk Road. The pebble passes from his
hand all the way to the Republic of Venice, the end of the Silk Road,
where a boy cherishes it and sees the value of this gift from a girl at
the end of the road"—— Provided by publisher.

Includes bibliographical references.

ISBN 978-1-59643-715-9 (hardcover : alk. paper)

1. Silk Road—Juvenile fiction. [1. Silk Road—Fiction. 2. Voyages and
travels—Fiction.] I. Title.

PZ7.C45235Si 2013

[E]—dc23

2012047600

Roaring Brook Press books are available for special promotions and premiums.
For details contact: Director of Special Markets, Holtzbrinck Publishers.

First edition 2013   Book design by Jennifer Browne
Printed in China by Toppan Leefung Printing Ltd., Dongguan City, Guangdong Province

1 3 5 7 9 10 8 6 4 2

A NOTE FROM THE AUTHOR

As a child, *One Thousand and One Nights* captivated my imagination. Scimitars, silks, perfumes, and genies filled my dreams. Over time, those dreams faded.

Then, three years ago, I received a request from the International Museum of Peace and Solidarity in Samarkand, Uzbekistan. Why was that name, Samarkand, so familiar? A few minutes of research told me—Samarkand was a stop along the trading routes known collectively as the Silk Road. But a few minutes of research is never enough. After a few hours of reading, the Silk Road had stolen my heart again. And so a story evolved, not quickly, but in one thousand and one nights.

Spring

The sun rose. Mei buzzed around her father, begging to travel to market with him.

"It's my job to trade our silk," he said. "It's your job to stay home and care for the silk worms."

Mei turned a jade pebble in her hand. Her father brought fantastic stories home from his travels; stories of monks and merchants, acrobats, pirates and thieves, those who traveled the long road between east and west. Mei longed to meet them all, to gather stories of her own.

"At least my pebble can go," she said. "A gift for a child at the end of the road."

"But it's only a pebble." Her father laughed.

"No," Mei answered. "It's cool like the stream where I found it, and green like the moss, and smooth like the water."

Mei's father smiled. "But I don't travel to the *end* of the road."

"You'll find a way," Mei said. "Everything is possible. And if a single pebble can travel to the end of the road, so can I!"

Summer

TURFAN

Mei's father turned the jade pebble in his hand. He'd sold his silk and bought a tiny square of blue glass that came from the west end of the road—thousands of miles away. A gift for Mei.

A Buddhist monk wandered by. "Why such a frown?" he asked.

"This single pebble. My daughter wants to send it west, to a child at the end of the road. But I must return home."

"I travel west, to Kashgar," the monk said. "I'll see that the pebble continues on."

"Please," Mei's father said, "say it's a gift from a girl . . . in the land where the sun rises."

Autumn

KASHGAR

The monk played his flute in the marketplace. Soldiers, traders, and pilgrims stopped a moment to listen. Only one young man, a sandalwood trader, lingered.

Later the two shared food while the monk told the story of the pebble. "But now I travel south," the monk said.

The sandalwood trader grinned. "I'm going west, I'll take—"

"*These*," the monk said. "The pebble *and* a flute. Gifts from . . . a girl in the land where the sun rises."

The sandalwood trader placed the gifts in his finest box to travel west.

Spring
SAMARKAND

Music and laughter rang from a far corner of the bazaar, where the sandalwood trader found a family performing acrobatics. When the music stopped only the sandalwood trader stayed to drop a coin in the payment bowl. Instantly, Laleh, the youngest daughter, began dancing. The sandalwood trader tried to dance, too, but the box in his belt kept slipping.

When the box fell open, Laleh's eyes widened.

"These treasures aren't mine," the sandalwood trader explained, and told the story. "And now I must return to India . . ."

"We'll carry the gifts west! To Baghdad!!" Laleh's father cried. "To Baghdad!" The family cheered.

"From a girl in the land where the sun rises," the sandalwood trader said.

Summer

BAGHDAD

The crowds in Baghdad cheered and made generous donations.
One night, after the crowd dispersed, Laleh found a tiny
carved elephant among the coins.

"For the box," she said.

"Lovely." A stranger's voice startled them all.

"A gift for a child at the west end of the road," Laleh said.

"Ahhhh." The stranger's eyes glimmered. "I'm traveling west myself . . ."

"Excellent. You can carry the treasure on," Laleh's father declared.

"It's a gift for a *child*." Laleh glared at the stranger. "From a girl in the land where the sun rises. And you must contribute."

The man offered a single stick of cinnamon. "I'm but a poor traveler," he growled. Reluctantly, Laleh released the box.

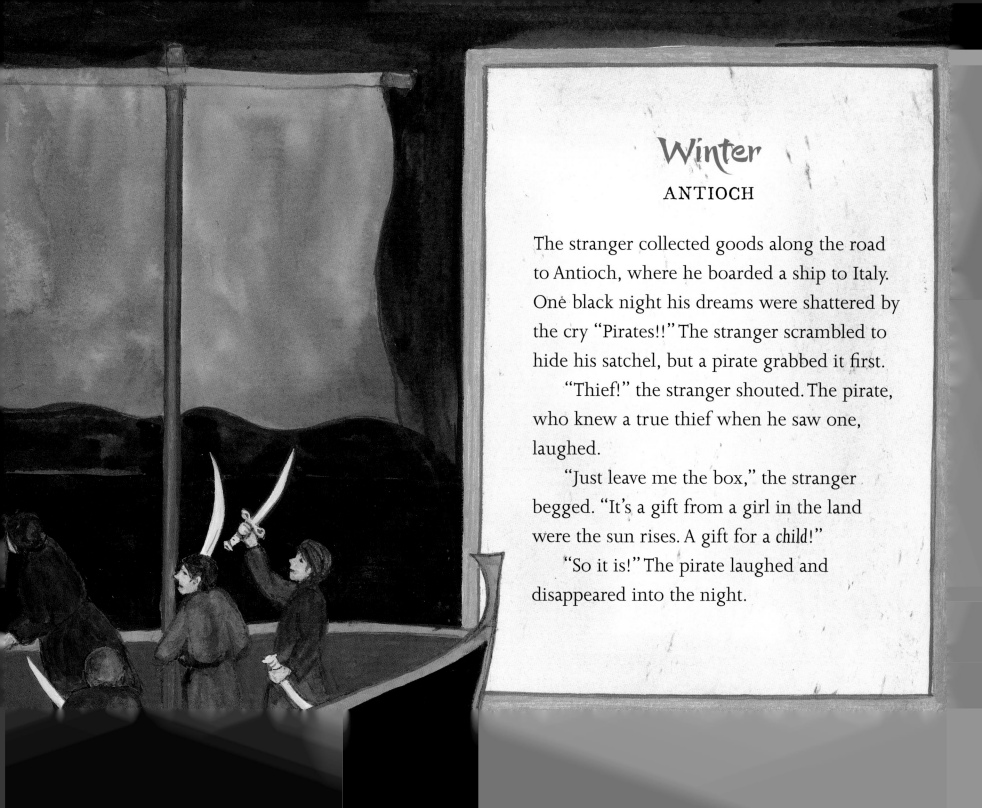

Winter

ANTIOCH

The stranger collected goods along the road to Antioch, where he boarded a ship to Italy. One black night his dreams were shattered by the cry "Pirates!!" The stranger scrambled to hide his satchel, but a pirate grabbed it first.

"Thief!" the stranger shouted. The pirate, who knew a true thief when he saw one, laughed.

"Just leave me the box," the stranger begged. "It's a gift from a girl in the land were the sun rises. A gift for a child!"

"So it is!" The pirate laughed and disappeared into the night.

Spring
TORCELLO

The pirate ship glided into its hiding place in the lagoon. Only one pirate stayed on the island. As he passed the church, tiny shards of blue glass, lost from the church's construction, glinted in the sun.

"Papa!" a boy yelled from down the road.

"Tommaso!" the pirate cried.

"Did you bring me anything?" asked Tommaso.

"Just a box."

Tommaso's eyes widened. He inhaled the sandalwood's perfume, tasted the cinnamon, admired the carved elephant, and tried a note on the flute. At last he found the pebble. "Ahhh, the best of all!"

"But it's only a pebble." His father laughed.

"No," Tommaso said. "It's cool like the breeze, and green like seaweed, and smooth like the water."

"From a girl in the land where the sun rises," the pirate said. Tommaso smiled, turned the pebble in his hand, and raised his face to the warmth of the sun.

Spring
NEAR CHANG'AN—852 AD

Four thousand miles away, Mei felt the spring sun on her face. She turned a tiny square of blue glass in her hand and recalled her father's words.

"You're strong and clever, Mei. It's not *impossible* that you may travel to the west end of the road, to the land where this glass began its journey."

"Not impossible?" Mei smiled. "If a tiny square of glass can travel to the end of the road, so can I."

A NOTE ON THE SILK ROAD

The name Silk Road refers to numerous trade routes that connected China with India, the Middle East, and the Mediterranean from around 206 BC through 1400 AD. Both land and sea routes were used to transport goods from east to west (silk, ceramics, plants, and tea), from west to east (gold, ivory, horses, and metal, as well as fine blown glass from the island of Torcello), and from the south to the north (cotton, perfume, and wood products).

Traders often traveled in horse or camel caravans as they crossed treacherous mountain ranges and deserts. Silk Road travelers endured sand storms, blazing heat, and freezing cold, as well as threat of attack by roving gangs of bandits. If all went well, traders would eventually reach an oasis marketplace, exchange their merchandise for gold or other goods, and return home. Although Marco Polo claimed to have traveled the full length of the Silk Road, traders generally traveled only part of the route.

The Silk Road was a channel for much more than traded commodities, however. Buddhist monks and missionaries spread their philosophy as they traveled, and technology made its way along the Silk Road as well. Paper, gunpowder, and the magnetic compass migrated from China to the west. Music traveled in all directions. String, wind, and percussion instruments, from both east and west, all had an influence on the development of one another.

Silk Road trade was a major influence in the development of the great empires and civilizations along the route, civilizations that literally paved the way for the modern world.

War and politics eventually divided empires along the Silk Road. Nomadic groups settled and formed mercantile states. By the year 1500 AD, silk was no longer traded along the Silk Road.

THE GIFTS

The Silk Road must certainly have been a feast for the senses. To highlight the sensory aspects of the Silk Road, I chose gifts that reflect all five senses. I'll leave it to you to identify each. These gifts accumulate as Mei's pebble passes from hand to hand.

MAP NOTE

During the Tang Dynasty, political borders moved frequently. Wars changed the size of kingdoms and many populations were nomadic. Like boundaries, some city names changed over time: Chang'an became Xi'an; Turfan is now called Turpan; and Antioch is Antakaya. Other city names—Torcello, Baghdad, Samarkand, and Kashgar— remain the same. The ninth century map at the beginning of this book is intended to give the reader a *sense* of land boundaries in the ninth century, despite the fact that the boundaries were not constant.

USEFUL WEBSITES

The Silk Road Project: silkroadproject.org
University of Washington:
depts.washington.edu/silkroad
University of California. Earth System Science:
ess.uci.edu/~oliver/silk.html

BIBLIOGRAPHY

Boulnois, Luce and Bradley Mayhew, *Silk Road: Monks, Warriors & Merchants*. Hong Kong: Airphoto International/Odyssey, 2012.

Whitfield, Susan. *Life along the Silk Road*. Berkeley: University of California, 1999.

Wood, Frances. *The Silk Road: Two Thousand Years in the Heart of Asia*. Berkeley: University of California, 2002.

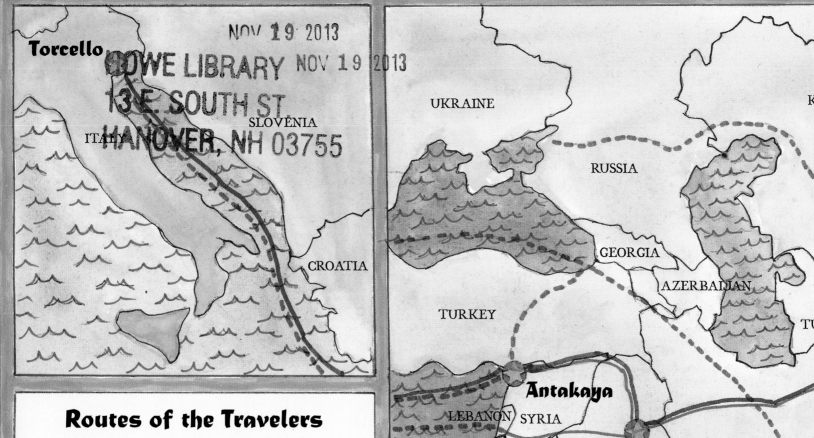

Torcello

SLOVENIA

ITALY

CROATIA

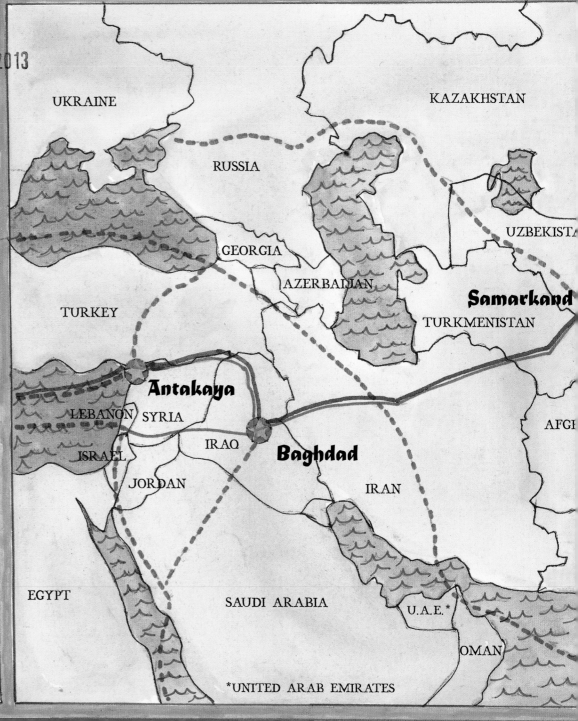

UKRAINE

KAZAKHSTAN

RUSSIA

UZBEKISTA

GEORGIA

AZERBAIJAN

Samarkand

TURKEY

TURKMENISTAN

Antakaya

LEBANON SYRIA

AFGH

IRAQ

Baghdad

ISRAEL

JORDAN

IRAN

EGYPT

SAUDI ARABIA

U.A.E.*

OMAN

*UNITED ARAB EMIRATES

Routes of the Travelers

——	Mei's father
——	monk
——	sandalwood trader
——	performing family
——	thief
——	pirate
——	the Silk Road
- - -	other trade routes